Hedgehogs Do Not Like Heights

Reading Ladder

Hedgehogs do not like heights.
I discovered that one afternoon last
summer. We had just had a picnic in
the garden when Lola disappeared.

I was sent to find her.

'Lola!' I called. No answer.

I looked in the potting shed. I looked down by the stream. I looked all over the garden. I couldn't see her anywhere.

6

Just as I was about to go back and
tell my mother, I heard her voice,
way above me.

'Hello Natalie! Where have you been?'
Lola said.

I looked up. There was Lola's smiling
face between the branches of the old
oak tree.

Peekaboo!

'Peekaboo!' she said.

'Lola!' I said. 'Come on
down. That tree is much
too high for you.'

Lola bit her lip and put the tip of her shoe on to the branch below her.

'No!' she said. 'I . . . I don't want to come down!'

'Are you stuck?' I asked.

'Not at all!' said Lola crossly. 'I'm busy.
I'm watching Fizzy Izzy getting married.
She's the tooth fairy, you know.'

Just then my mother appeared.
'Lola!' she said. 'Come down
at once!'

Oops!

'I'm sorry, Mummy,' said Lola. 'I can't come down. You see . . . you see . . . Fizzy Izzy is getting married and she invited me to her wedding.'

'Are you stuck?' Mum said, looking up
at Lola.

Lola shook her head crossly.

'No, I'm not stuck!' she said. Then she
turned back to me.

'Oh Natalie!' she said. 'Fizzy Izzy is marrying Solomon Spider and she has the most beautiful dress made out of spider's web. I wish you could see it.'

My mother called my father.

Dad got the ladder.

He climbed up shakily,

one step,

two steps,

then he stopped.

I can't look!

'Are you coming to see the wedding
Daddy?' Lola asked.

'No!' said Dad. 'I . . . I feel a bit dizzy.
I think I should come down.'

My mum was very cross. She kicked
off her shoes and started up the ladder
herself but the ladder was too short.
'Lola!' my mother said. 'Be a good
child and climb down. Put your foot
on the branch below you.'

'Oh Mummy! I can't leave now. A nasty goblin has just arrived at the wedding. He's very angry because he wasn't invited. I think he's going to cast a spell.'

ickory Pickory diddley doo

With that, Lola disappeared into the tree again. My father called the fire brigade. We could hear its bell ringing long before we saw it.

CLANG CLANG

The fireman stood looking up into the tree.

'Don't worry,' he said. 'We'll have her down in a jiffy.'

No problemo!

Just then, Lola looked out through the branches.

'Are you stuck, little girl?' said the fireman.

Lola pressed her lips together.

'I am NOT stuck,' she said. 'Grim the
Goblin is throwing acorns at the bride
and groom, and Solomon is getting

very annoyed.'

'Grim the Goblin?' said the fire chief and

his whole face creased into one big frown.

'What sort of nonsense is that?'

25

Just then, an acorn hit him squarely
on the nose.

'Ouch!' said the fireman. 'My nose!
My nose!'

My father called the ambulance.

Nee naw! Nee naw!

The ambulance people brought a
stretcher but the fireman refused to
lie down.

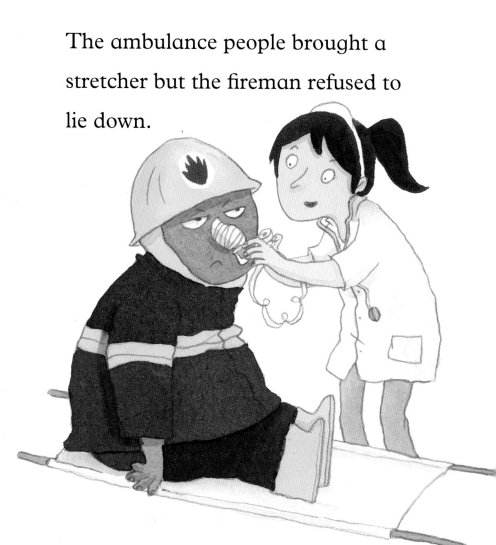

'I'm fine!' he yelled at the ambulance
nurse. 'I don't want to go anywhere!
Leave me alone!'

'That's just what Grim the Goblin said,' Lola called, from the tree. 'He refused to go home and leave the

wedding in peace. That's why the spiders tied him up with miles of smooth, silky threads. And now he can't as much as twitch his nose!'

'Well we can't tie the fire chief up,' said the doctor, frowning. 'We don't have any rope!'

'Oh no!' Lola said. 'You won't believe what's just happened!'

What?

What?

What

'What?' I said.

'What?' said my mum and dad.

'What?' said the fireman, the doctor
and the nurse.

'A nasty little squirrel just bit through the threads that were keeping Grim the Goblin all tied up. Grim escaped

WHOOSH!

and put a spell on Fizzy Izzy, turning
her into a hedgehog. And hedgehogs do
NOT like heights. Poor Izzy is terrified.'

'What are you going to do?'

I shouted to Lola.

'It's OK!' said Lola. 'Rubella the Witch
has just arrived on her broomstick!'
'Oh no!' I said.

'Oh yes!' said Lola. 'You see, Rubella is Izzy's second cousin, once and a half removed, and she just turned Izzy back into Izzy!'

'Hurray!' said the fireman, forgetting about his nose for a minute.

'Wait!' said Lola. 'Rubella's just turned Grim into an acorn.

'Solomon's made a catapult out of some
web and . . . wheeee! There he goes!
Did you see him fly through the sky?'

WHEEEE!

I squinted up at the blue sky but I
couldn't see a thing.
'Yes!' said the fireman.
'I saw him!'

Just then, I had a great idea.

'Lola!' I said. 'Why don't we all go up there with you and watch the rest of the wedding? Then we could help you climb down when it's all over.'

'Oh yes!' said the fireman. 'I love weddings.'

'No!' said Lola. 'Do not come up! Izzy and Solomon wouldn't like it. They're very shy. I'm not even going to stay and I'm invited. I'm . . . I'm coming down right away.'

Lola put the tip of her toe on the branch below her. Then, the rest of her toe and all of her foot. Everyone cheered as Lola climbed down, down, down and out of the big oak tree.

I climbed up later but I didn't see any of the wedding party. I supposed they had all gone home. Just as I started to climb back down, I felt something silky tickle my ankle.